AGATHA

Anna Pignataro

For IF, there's no one else like you.
Thank you to Susanne Gervay for your words of wisdom
and Karen Tayleur for making a dream come true.

~Anna Pignataro

little bee books

An imprint of Bonnier Publishing Group
853 Broadway, New York, New York 10003
Copyright © 2015 by Anna Pignataro.
First published in Australia by The Five Mile Press.
This little bee books edition, 2015.
Manufactured in China 0615 PP
First Edition 2 4 6 8 10 9 7 5 3 1
Library of Congress Control Number: 2015934159
ISBN 978-1-4998-0096-8

www.littlebeebooks.com
www.bonnierpublishing.com

AGATHA

Anna Pignataro

little bee books

Once upon a time, not so long ago,
Albert and Victoria waited for the arrival
of a very special person.

Just as the leaves were falling, Agatha was born.
She had her mother's ears and her father's nose.

When Agatha's family were all together, she didn't quite fit in.

And when Agatha started kindergarten, she realized
she was a little different from everyone else.

At first it wasn't easy to make new friends.
Agatha tried extra hard...

even when George teased her.

One day, Miss Tibble said that, like snowflakes and stars, everybody was special in their own way.

"I think I am special because I can make delicious cakes," she said. "Who's next?"

Agatha felt nervous.

She liked soccer,
    but George liked it more.

She was good at singing, but May was better.

She could karate kick,
        but Yoko could kick higher.

Agatha wasn't sure what made her special.

She thought that if she could be very, very quiet
then everyone would forget that she was there,
and she wouldn't have to say anything.

So, when George was dribbling his soccer ball, Agatha shut her eyes and pretended she was somewhere else.

While May was singing, Agatha crept away.

When Yoko was doing karate kicks, Agatha hid.

"Where's Agatha?" May asked when everyone had finished showing what made them special.

The class searched everywhere, but no one could find her.

Yoko and George looked worried, and May started to cry.
Agatha felt awful. She didn't want May to cry, and
she didn't want anyone to be worried.

REST

"I'm here," said Agatha.

"There you are!" said Miss Tibble. "Agatha, it's your turn.
Now tell us, what makes you special?"
Agatha shrugged.

"Maybe she's special because she's so good at hiding?" suggested George.
Everyone laughed.

"I think Agatha is special," said Miss Tibble,
"because she is a very good helper."

"I think Agatha's special because she is the best
at making funny faces!" said Yoko.

"I know why you are special, Agatha," said May.

"Because you are the best at being Agatha.
No one else is a better Agatha than you!"